THE eXTREME Team

#6
INTO THE DANGER ZONE

Text by Stephanie Peters
Illustrated by Michael Koelsch

LITTLE, BROWN AND COMPANY
New York Boston

Little, Brown and Company

Time Warner Book Group
1271 Avenue of the Americas, New York, NY 10020
Visit our Web site at www.lb-kids.com

www.mattchristopher.com

First Edition

Library of Congress Cataloging-in-Publication Data
Peters, Stephanie True.
Into the danger zone / Matt Christopher ; text by Stephanie Peters ; illustrated by Michael Koelsch. – 1st ed.
p. cm. – (The extreme team ; #6)
Summary: When an old friend comes to visit, Charlie is not at all happy with the changes he sees – especially when Rick gets reckless on his snowboard, chasing X and some of Charlie's other friends off the slopes.
ISBN 0-316-76266-0 (hc) / ISBN 0-316-76267-9 (pb)
[1. Friendship – Fiction. 2. Snowboarding – Fiction. 3. Skateboarding – Fiction. 4. Remarriage – Fiction. 5. Safety – Fiction.] I. Christopher, Matt . II. Koelsch, Michael, ill. III. Title. IV. Series.
PZ7.P441833In 2005 2003023757
[Fic] – dc22

10 9 8 7 6 5 4 3 2 1

PHX (hc)

COM-MO (pb)

Printed in the United States of America

CHAPTER ONE

"Man, I can almost *taste* the warm weather, can't you?"

Charlie Abbott spun around on his skateboard and grinned at Jonas Malloy. "I hear you, dude. I like snowboarding and all, but it's been a long winter. I'm craving some action on the half-pipe and rails!" He pushed off and started moving down the sidewalk again. "How many more weeks until the skatepark reopens?"

Jonas groaned. "Alison said at least three. No exceptions." Alison Lee was the teenager who ran the local skatepark and the snowboarding slope behind it. She set the rules for both and made sure everyone followed them.

"That means mid-April at the earliest," Charlie said. He dodged around a dirty pile of old snow. "I'm not sure I'll be able to wait that long!"

"No kidding. But what can you do? Rules are rules."

Charlie heard someone shout his name. He and Jonas both stopped as Xavier "X" McSweeney boarded up beside them. He was clutching a newspaper.

"You will not believe this!" he cried. He thrust the paper into Jonas's hands and pointed to an advertisement.

Jonas's jaw dropped. "No *way!*" he exclaimed. He handed the paper to Charlie and double high-fived X.

Charlie read the ad out loud. "'Rocket Robert and the Shred Devils to appear one night only!'" He gave the paper back to Jonas. "Who's Rocket Robert, and what's a Shred Devil?"

Jonas and X stared at him in amazement. "Have you been living in a cave?" X said. "Rocket Robert is only the best skateboarder in the country! He and the Shred Devils – the other boarders and inline skaters in his group – are on a worldwide tour. They're going to

put on a show here!" He turned to Jonas. "Remember when we saw Rocket Robert two years ago?"

Jonas grinned. "You and me and Bizz were just getting good at boarding," he said. Belicia "Bizz" Juarez was another friend who loved skateboarding. "We kept doing our moves in the stadium parking lot, hoping Rocket would see us and ask us to be in the show!"

X cracked up. "Yeah! And we had that one move we thought was killer, where we did that thing with our arms –"

"– and that other thing with our legs!" Jonas finished. He flailed his limbs, laughing so hard he almost lost his balance. "Mark and Savannah thought we were crazy!" he added, referring to their pals Mark Goldstein and Savannah Smith.

Charlie couldn't help smiling with them, even though he had no idea what they were talking about. He had moved into town less than a year ago. He was still getting to know X and Jonas and the others, while they had known each other almost their entire lives. Sometimes he envied them their long friendships.

"So when is this Rocket Robert show, anyway?" he asked.

"Next Saturday," X answered, "so we gotta get our tickets soon!"

"Next Saturday? I don't know if I can go!" Jonas and X looked at Charlie questioningly. "My old friend Patrick is coming to visit next Friday after school. His mom just got remarried, and my parents are going to meet her new husband for the first time. They're staying the whole weekend."

"So bring ol' Pat along, dude. You can't miss Rocket Robert!" Jonas cried.

X echoed Jonas. "Yeah, it won't be as much fun if you're not there!"

Charlie's heart warmed. So what if he hadn't known them all his life? He was still their good friend.

CHAPTER TWO

"So who is this guy Patrick, anyway?" X asked as they continued boarding down the sidewalk.

Charlie popped his board into the air, did a kick flip, and landed safely back on the board again. "I hung out with him a few years ago," he replied. "He's a good guy. Went through a pretty tough time when his parents got divorced."

Jonas nodded as if he understood, and Charlie remembered that his parents, too, were divorced.

"Anyway, I haven't seen him since we moved away a year and a half ago. We kept in touch through e-mails and were going to get together, but then my family moved again, to this town. I haven't heard from him lately. Guess he's been busy with his mom's wedding and the new stepdad and all."

"Is he into extreme?" Jonas wanted to know.

"Way into it. In fact, he and his dad taught me a lot about boarding, like riding the rails and stuff." He zigzagged onto the road, then jumped his board back up to the sidewalk. "That's why I wish the skatepark was going to be open when he's here. He'd love it. Think Alison would let us in, just for a day?"

"Doubt it," came X's immediate reply. "She told me the equipment has to be checked out first. She was worried the half-pipe might have been damaged over the winter or something."

Charlie was disappointed, but he understood. Alison had to make sure the park was safe, after all. If she didn't, and someone got hurt, she'd be in major trouble.

The boys boarded in silence for a while, popping wheelies and ollies and practicing their kick flips. They

were so intent on what they were doing, they didn't notice that dark clouds had rolled in and the temperature had dropped. Only when Jonas's teeth started chattering did they realize it was about to snow.

"C'mon, my house is right around the corner!" Jonas cried as the first flakes fell. Laughing, the three boys picked up their boards and ran as fast as they could to the Malloys'.

"Dad!" Jonas bellowed as he burst through the kitchen door. "Rocket Robert is coming to town! Can we get tickets? If we can, I promise I'll shovel the driveway and the sidewalk and –"

Mr. Malloy emerged from his office. He worked at home, creating and designing video games. Charlie and his friends thought it was the coolest job ever.

"I'm one step ahead of you," Mr. Malloy said. He dug a hand into his shirt pocket and pulled out an envelope. Inside were twelve tickets to the Rocket Robert show. He handed X and Charlie two tickets each. "One for you, and one for one of your parents," he explained. "Your folks can fight over which parent gets to go. I'll give the other tickets to Bizz, Mark, and Savannah later today."

X and Jonas whooped. "Thanks, Dad!" Jonas cried.

Mr. Malloy smiled. "You can still do the shoveling, though," he said to Jonas as he disappeared back into his office.

Charlie stared at the tickets in his hand and sighed. "I sure hope I get to use these," he said.

During dinner that night, Charlie's mother turned to him and said, "Oh, by the way, Jonas's father called earlier to make sure it was okay to buy us tickets for the Rocket Robert show. Sounds like fun to me."

"Um, but Mom, what about Pat?" Charlie said.

To his relief, she started laughing. "Well, for heaven's sake, he can use my ticket! I'm sure Mr. Malloy or one of the other parents won't mind looking out for you boys that night. Your father and I will have a nice visit with Pat's folks instead."

"Hold on a second." Mr. Abbott was frowning. "You seem to be forgetting something, my dear."

Charlie held his breath.

"That ticket was supposed to go to *you* *or* to me," Mr. Abbott continued solemnly. "What makes you so sure *I* don't want to use it to see Rocket Robert?"

CHAPTER THREE

It took Charlie a split second to realize that his father was joking. His mother threw a balled-up napkin at her husband and the three of them started laughing.

"Had you going there for a moment, didn't I?" his father chortled.

Just then, the phone rang. Mrs. Abbott excused herself and answered it. She spoke to the caller for a few minutes, then hung up and returned to the table.

"That was Pat's mother. She wanted to know if she should bring his skateboard, his snowboard, his inline skates, or all three. I told her just the snowboard since it's snowing again. That okay, Charlie?"

He nodded. "If it sticks to the ground, the slope should be good for boarding."

He hoped it would be. Otherwise, he wasn't sure what he was going to do with Pat for two whole days. They had been good friends a couple of years earlier. But Charlie had moved twice since then, and they'd lost touch. He didn't want to admit it, but he was a little nervous about seeing Pat again. What if they didn't have anything in common anymore? He figured snowboarding together would help them get reacquainted.

Luckily, the snow didn't melt. In fact, every day after school that week Charlie met his friends at the top of the slope. The conditions were mint.

"Ya-HOO!" Bizz shouted as she started her first run on Thursday afternoon. She crisscrossed the hill smoothly, leaving winding lines in the snow behind her. Leaning over the nose of his board to make himself go faster, Jonas followed her.

"I'm looking forward to meeting your friend," Savannah said as she waited her turn. When Jonas was halfway down, she took off. Savannah moved more slowly and cautiously than either Jonas or Bizz. She was still learning to snowboard, and even though she'd improved a lot since the beginning of the winter, she wasn't one hundred percent confident yet. Still, she enjoyed boarding and wasn't afraid to try new things. Charlie admired her for that.

Then it was his turn. After adjusting his goggles and hat, he stepped into his bindings and snapped them on tight. Then he gave a little hop and started down the slope. The hill wasn't that long but it was plenty steep. Charlie picked up speed, zigzagging in quick turns, making sure to keep an eye out for any other boarders or sledders. The last thing he wanted was a collision!

He made it to the end and stopped himself with a sharp twist that sent a spray of snow into the air. Then he unsnapped his bindings, picked up his board, and joined other kids making their way up the side of the hill. He caught up with Savannah.

"So, what's your friend like?" she asked.

"When I last saw him he was kind of short and skinny," Charlie answered.

"Like me, you mean?" Jonas joined them. "I like the guy already."

Charlie grinned. "Yeah, and I remember he was fearless, too, but he knew how to keep it real, you know?"

"Again, like me!"

Savannah rolled her eyes. "Just what we *don't* need – two Jonases!"

Laughing, the three friends made their way to the top of the hill. One after another, they took off again. Charlie was feeling great. The snowboarding was awesome, and his friends were talking about Pat as if he were one of them. If things kept going this well, the weekend visit was going to be a breeze.

Unfortunately, the next afternoon, it felt more like a tornado.

CHAPTER FOUR

Charlie stood next to his parents in the driveway. Patrick and his mother and stepfather had just driven up. Pat was the first one out of the car.

"Yo, dude, how's it going?"

Charlie couldn't answer at first. He was too busy staring at his friend.

"My goodness," he heard his mother murmur, "Patrick certainly has sprouted!"

"Sprouted" wasn't exactly how Charlie would have described the change in his friend. "Doubled in size" was more like it.

When Charlie had last seen him, the top of Pat's head had barely reached Charlie's shoulder. Now he

stood a full half-head taller than Charlie! He'd gained weight, too. Next to him, Charlie felt like a Chihuahua in the presence of a Saint Bernard.

"H-hey there, bro," he finally stammered. "Long time no see."

Pat socked him in the shoulder so hard that Charlie's eyes watered. As Charlie rubbed the sore spot, Pat's mother called over to them.

"Rick, why don't you and Charlie bring your things into the house?"

"Rick"? Charlie thought. *Since when is he called "Rick"?*

"C'mon, man," Pat – Rick – said. "Help me get my stuff."

Happy to be doing something, Charlie hurried to the car. Rick's mother popped the trunk and Rick pulled out a duffel bag. Underneath it was a gleaming snowboard.

"Wow, that's a beauty!" Charlie said with admiration as he carefully took it from the trunk.

"Pretty slick, huh? Too bad I couldn't bring my skateboard and blades, but Joe said I had to leave them at home."

"Joe?"

Rick jerked a thumb behind him. Only then did Charlie notice the tall man standing with Rick's mother.

"Oh, so that's your new dad?" Charlie asked.

"No!" The sudden anger in Rick's voice surprised Charlie. "He's my mom's new husband, *not* my dad."

"Oh, right." Embarrassed, Charlie tried to think of something to say. His mother saved him.

"After you get Pat – er, Rick – settled in, maybe you can take him to the slope, Charlie," she suggested. "Then tomorrow you can bring him to the skatepark."

Rick looked at Joe accusingly. "I thought you said the skatepark was closed!"

"It is," Mrs. Abbott hastened to say, looking from Rick to Joe and back again, "but that doesn't mean you can't take a look at it, right?"

Charlie held his breath as Rick glared at Joe a moment longer. Then suddenly the anger melted from

Rick's face and he turned to Mrs. Abbott with an angelic smile.

"You're absolutely right, Mrs. Abbott," he said politely. He hoisted his duffel onto his shoulder. "Charlie, can you show me your room now?" He gave the four adults one more smile, then turned to walk inside.

As Charlie fell in next to Rick, his old friend nudged him in the ribs.

"Maybe we'll find a way to check out that park for real, huh, bro?" he whispered. With a sly grin, he hoisted his duffel bag higher on his shoulder and opened the front door to the house.

Charlie stared after him. *What does he mean, "for real"?* he wondered. Suddenly, he had a sneaking suspicion that Patrick, or Rick, or whatever he called himself, had changed more than his size in the last two years.

CHAPTER FIVE

An hour later, Charlie and Rick climbed into the back of Mrs. Abbott's car. As Mrs. Abbott started the engine, Joe opened a door and stuck his head inside.

"You be careful out there," he said to Rick, "okay?" He straightened up and slammed the door shut.

Rick rolled his eyes and stared out the window. He didn't move from that position until they reached the slope.

Charlie looked around for his friends. When he didn't see any of them, he breathed a sigh of relief. He realized that he'd been hoping he wouldn't have to introduce Rick to them. Not yet, anyway.

Rick took a look around. "*This* is where you

board?" he said with disdain. "Man, you barely start down when you run out of hill!"

Charlie swallowed an angry reply. "Actually, I've had some sweet runs here. And it's a good hill if you want to practice tricks and stuff."

Rick looked unconvinced. "Well, compared to the slopes I've been on, this one is really lame. And crowded, too, which is hard to believe given its total lameness. But I'll give it a try, I guess."

Don't do me any favors, Charlie felt like saying. But he didn't. Stunned as he was by Rick's rudeness, he knew it would be a very long and uncomfortable weekend if he challenged him. So instead of replying, he trudged up the hill behind Rick.

Alison Lee was monitoring the slope as usual. Praying that Rick didn't repeat his opinion of the hill, Charlie introduced them to each other.

"Rick, this is Alison. She's in charge of the slope and the skatepark. Rick's visiting for the weekend."

Before his eyes, Rick's attitude changed dramatically. "Nice to meet you," he said, his voice oily smooth. "This hill looks very challenging. I can tell you do a good job keeping everyone safe."

Alison glanced at Charlie, then replied in an equally polite voice, "Thank you, Rick. I hope you enjoy your stay here."

"I'm sure I will," Rick replied. "Is it okay for me to try going down now?"

Alison nodded. Rick strapped on his board and, with a little wave, began his run. He moved slowly, almost cautiously, swooping right and left with neat little turns.

"Interesting friend you have there," Alison murmured to Charlie. Just then, her walkie-talkie gave a beep. She unhooked it from her belt and spoke into it.

"Go ahead. Over." A voice crackled back. Alison listened intently, then said, "On my way. Over and out," and clicked off.

"They need me at the Community Center," she said, fastening on her board. "A pipe burst in the women's bathroom. I have to cover the front desk while they clean up the mess."

"Are you going to close the slope?" Charlie asked.

Alison shook her head. "I shouldn't be too long. But take this." She thrust her walkie-talkie into Charlie's hands. "If anything should happen, give me a shout, okay?"

"But-but –," Charlie sputtered.

"Look, I'd rather not leave you in charge, believe me!" Alison said. "But I think you'll be okay until I get back. Everyone here knows the rules."

Practically everyone, Charlie wanted to remind her as she took off down the slope. He was staring at the walkie-talkie as if it might bite him when Rick returned to the top of the hill.

"What's that?"

Reluctantly, Charlie explained the situation.

Rick gave a slow smile. "So-o-o-o," he said, "she's gone for a bit, huh? That's good. That's ve-e-e-ery good!"

Charlie was instantly on his guard. "Why do you say that?"

Rick just winked. "I gotta go to the bathroom.

See ya." He took off down the slope. But unlike the last run, when he knew Alison was watching, this one was far from slow and smooth. He darted in and out, crossing in front of other boarders and nearly toppling a few.

Watching him, Charlie gripped the walkie-talkie so tightly that his fingers ached.

"Who was that loser?" a voice beside him demanded. It was X. "You should throw him off the hill!"

CHAPTER SIX

"Me?" Charlie's voice came out in a squeak. "Why should I be the one to throw him off?"

X pointed at the walkie-talkie in Charlie's hand. "Because Alison put you in charge, you goofball. I saw her at the bottom of the hill just now and she told me."

"Yeah, but she didn't say anything about me throwing anyone off, did she?" Charlie said desperately.

"Well, no. But one of us could call over to the Community Center and tell them about that nostril slug." X reached for the walkie-talkie.

Charlie jerked it away. "Or," he said, "I could just,

you know, talk to the kid. Maybe he doesn't know the rules."

X looked at him for a long moment. Then he shrugged. "Maybe. But if you ask me, the guy looks like a total pea brain. And until he clears out, I'm staying off the hill and telling Jonas and the others to do the same." He picked up his board, then looked over his shoulder at Charlie. "If you're not going to report the guy, at least warn anyone going down the slope to look out for him, okay?"

Charlie watched his friend walk down the side of the hill. Every so often X stopped and spoke to some kids – telling them about Rick, Charlie figured. Many turned and left the hill like X. By the time Rick returned from the bathroom, there were half as many boarders and sledders as before.

When Rick made it to the top of the hill he was grinning. "Works every time!" he said gleefully.

"What works every time?" Charlie asked.

Rick smirked. "All it takes is one wild run to clear

the 'fraidy cats from a hill. One more should take care of the rest. Then you and I can board to our hearts' content, my friend!"

Charlie was appalled. Without thinking, he raised the walkie-talkie to his mouth and pushed the signal button.

Rick grabbed Charlie's arm. "What are you going to do," he said in a challenging voice, "tattle on me? Never figured you would turn in an old friend."

The two boys stared at each other until a crackle from the walkie-talkie broke Charlie's gaze.

"Everything okay, Charlie? Over." Alison asked.

Charlie hesitated. He knew he should report Rick. But if he did, the rest of the weekend would be a disaster.

And he is only here for the weekend, he told himself. *If I can just get through these next few days, I won't have to see him again – not if I have anything to say about it!*

Feeling like a traitor, he clicked back on. "Sorry,

Alison, I – I hit the button by mistake. Everything's fine here. Over and out."

With a low laugh, Rick leaned forward on his board and disappeared down the hill, leaving Charlie shivering at the top – and not just with the cold.

CHAPTER SEVEN

That night, at home, Charlie tried his best to be civil to Rick. But it wasn't easy. One minute Rick was telling Mrs. Abbott how much he was enjoying his supper; the next, he was jabbing Charlie under the table, rolling his eyes and pretending that the lasagna was making him sick.

But Charlie was the one who really felt sick. It wasn't just Rick's behavior that was bothering him, however. His own behavior on top of the hill was also causing his stomach to do flip-flops.

What else could I have done? he kept asking himself. Unfortunately, the answer was the same every time. He should have stood up to Rick. Now it was too late.

The only thing that comforted him was that no one had been hurt by Rick's snowboarding antics. But he knew it easily could have been otherwise. What if Savannah had been boarding during Rick's wild run? She might not have been able to get out of his way. And what would happen if Rick wanted to go snowboarding again tomorrow? Saturdays were always the busiest days on the hill. Would Rick pull his trick again to try to drive people away?

These questions were still racing through his brain as he lay in bed that night. He didn't think he'd ever fall asleep. But he must have, for he was later woken by the sound of rain lashing against the side of the house. As he listened to it, he smiled. Rain would wash away the snow. No snow, no snowboarding. With a sigh of relief, he fell back to sleep.

The next thing he knew, it was morning. He peeked out the window. Sure enough, last night's rain had washed away most of the snow.

"Good morning, buddy." Charlie walked into the

kitchen to find Rick having breakfast with the four grown-ups. "Did you look outside? Those sidewalks are clear as can be. Too bad I didn't bring my skateboard or my inlines."

Charlie forced a smile, then went to the cupboard to get a bowl for his cereal. As he reached up, the phone rang. Charlie answered it.

"Yo, bro, whaddya know?"

"Hey, Jonas, what's up?"

"Missed you at the slope yesterday. I was on my way up when X told me some crazy kid was causing trouble, so I bagged it," Jonas answered. "Anyway, what are you doing today? Did your friend Pat ever show up? X said he didn't see him with you yesterday."

Charlie turned his back to the table. "Yeah, he's here," he muttered.

"So when do we get to meet him?" Jonas asked. "Maybe we could all go skateboarding together today."

Charlie's mind whirled. He still wasn't sure he wanted Jonas and the others to meet Rick. What if X recognized Rick as the menace from the slope? And

he hadn't forgotten Rick's little comment about checking out the skatepark even though it was closed. He decided it would be safer overall if he and Rick just stayed close to home.

"Uh, he doesn't have his board or inlines with him," he replied. "Listen, maybe we'll catch up with you later, okay?"

"Well, duh, of course you will," Jonas said with a laugh. "We're all going to the Rocket Robert show tonight, remember?"

Charlie sagged against the counter. He'd totally forgotten about Rocket Robert. He mumbled something to Jonas, then hung up, wondering if things could possibly get any worse.

They did.

"Charlie," his mother said brightly, "Rick just had a terrific idea."

"Yes," Rick said just as brightly. "If you use your inline skates and lend me your skateboard, we could take a ride. Oh, and hey," he added, as if it had suddenly occurred to him, "you could show me the skatepark!"

CHAPTER EIGHT

Charlie tried his best to come up with an excuse for why the plan wouldn't work. Before he could, however, Joe spoke up.

"Rick, perhaps it would be better if you boys didn't do any extreme sports today. It'd be a shame if one of you got hurt and couldn't go to the Rocket Robert show tonight."

Rick shot Joe a venomous look. But when he replied, his voice was even. "Hmm, good point, Joe. But of course we'll be wearing our helmets and protective gear. And besides, I'm always careful." He turned to Charlie. "How about we let Charlie decide?"

Feeling trapped, Charlie stared at his feet. He

wanted to say no but knew he couldn't. So he mumbled, "'S'okay with me."

Later, in the garage, he secured his inline skates onto his feet and rolled his skateboard to Rick. Instead of heading in the direction of the skatepark, Charlie steered Rick toward the opposite side of town. He hoped the other boy would get tired and give up on wanting to see the park. He should have known better.

After twenty minutes of riding on sidewalks and around dead-end street circles, Rick stopped short. "Listen, are you taking me on a joyride or something? Because I gotta tell you, this ain't very joyful. Where's that skatepark?"

Charlie knew he'd lost. "Okay, okay," he muttered. "C'mon, it's this way."

Fifteen minutes later, they stopped outside the short chain-link fence that surrounded the skatepark. Charlie saw Rick glance at the padlocked gate. But to his relief, Rick seemed content simply to look at the park's equipment from where they stood.

"Bet those rails are perfect to grind on," Rick said. His voice was wistful. "And that half-pipe looks awesome." He turned to Charlie, smiling. "You remember when we were first learning to ride the pipe?"

Charlie blinked in surprise. A strange transformation seemed to have come over Rick while he was looking at the park. Gone were the mocking tone, the angry voice. It was as if "Rick" had suddenly vanished and been replaced with "Pat," the friend Charlie had known two years earlier.

"Course I remember," Charlie replied softly. "If it hadn't been for you and your dad pushing me to keep at it, I never would have conquered that pipe."

"Yeah," his friend said, "those were good times." And then, just like that, his voice altered again, hardening and turning bitter. "Too bad everything had to change."

For a split second, Charlie thought Rick was referring to the fact that he, Charlie, had moved away. Then he realized what Rick was really angry about.

"I – I was sorry to hear your parents were getting divorced," he said in a low voice. "Your dad is really cool. Do you get to see him much?"

Rick picked up a rock and threw it as hard as he could. Charlie heard it bounce against the half-pipe. "Not enough," he finally answered. "I was supposed to spend weekends with him. But after the wedding, Mom asked Dad to let me stay with Joe and her so I could get to know Joe better. Like I really want to do *that*." He picked up another rock and hurled it even harder.

"Joe's not so great, huh?"

Rick snorted. "The guy's a loser!" he cried. "Every time I get ready to go snowboarding or skateboarding, he's on my case about safety this and be careful that! Fat lot he knows about it! He's never even bothered to come watch me do my thing! Well, I'm sick and tired of him trying to control my life. I'll show him."

And before Charlie could stop him, Rick had

tossed Charlie's skateboard over the fence and had leaped after it.

"Rick! Wait!" Charlie yelled. But it was too late.

Skateboard in hand, Rick headed straight for the half-pipe.

CHAPTER NINE

Charlie fumbled with the straps on his inline skates and kicked his feet free.

I've got to go after him! he thought frantically.

But he's bigger than you, a voice inside him argued. *How will you stop him?*

Meanwhile, Rick had made it to the bottom of the half-pipe. Suddenly, something X had said came into Charlie's mind.

The half-pipe might have been damaged over the winter.

Panic rising, Charlie vaulted the fence, landing hard on the other side in his stocking feet. As he started to run toward the half-pipe, he remembered the cell phone his parents always made him take along when he went out. He dug it out of his coat pocket and started to dial his home number.

Then he stopped and hit the hang-up button. If he told his parents what was happening, they'd tell Rick's mother and Joe. Somehow, Charlie didn't think having Joe here would help matters. He dialed the number of the Community Center instead. Out of the corner of his eye, he saw Rick reach the deck of the half-pipe.

Please be there, he prayed as the phone rang. When Alison picked up, his heart leaped. He hurriedly explained what was happening.

"I'll be right there," she said. "Do what you can to stop him!"

Splashing through puddles from the previous night's rain, Charlie ran as quickly as he could to the half-pipe. He was too late. Rick had started his run. Charlie could only hope that X had been wrong, that the half-pipe was fine.

At first, it seemed that everything would be okay.

Rick zipped down one side of the pipe and up the other, caught good air, turned, and zoomed down again toward the other side.

Then something happened. At the bottom of the half-pipe, the skateboard suddenly gave a jerk. As Charlie watched helplessly, Rick was hurled into the air. He smacked against the incline in front of him and slid to a stop at the bottom. The skateboard came to a rest next to him, its wheels spinning.

Charlie raced to his friend's side.

"Rick? Rick!" he cried. "Can you hear me?"

For a moment there was no reply. Then Rick groaned and opened his eyes.

"Wha– what happened?" he said groggily.

"You wiped out, man," Charlie answered, relief washing through his body.

Rick sat up slowly. "No way, bro, I never wipe out. There's something wrong with your board." He sounded stronger with every word. "A loose wheel or something. I felt it give."

Charlie grabbed his board and carefully spun the

wheels. "They seem fine to me," he said, puzzled. "So what happened?"

"Maybe this has something to do with it." It was Alison. She picked up a rock from the bottom of the pipe. Images of Rick throwing rocks into the skatepark – of one of the rocks bouncing near the half-pipe – flashed across Charlie's brain.

"It must have landed *in* the pipe after Rick threw it. Then my skateboard hit it and threw him," he mused.

Alison had been inspecting Rick for any injuries. Satisfied that he was okay, she helped him to his feet. "Well," she said, "that answers the question of how the rock got into the half-pipe. But what I really want to know" – she looked from one boy to the other, then settled her gaze on Rick – "is what *you* were doing in the half-pipe?"

CHAPTER TEN

It was Charlie who answered. "I – I think maybe I know." He turned to Rick. "From that wild run you took down the slopes yesterday – sorry, Alison, I should have told you about that – and from the way you were acting during dinner last night, I thought you'd turned into a real jerk."

Rick didn't say anything.

"But you know what I think now?" Charlie continued. "I think you're just angry – at your mom, at Joe, and especially at your dad. And you're taking it out on anyone you can. Me, the kids at the slope, even my mom's lasagna!"

Rick managed a small smile. But the smile faded

when Charlie added, "And today, you took it out on yourself."

Rick was silent for a few moments. "I just can't believe my mom married that loser," he finally said, "and that they're keeping me from seeing my dad. It all stinks."

Alison laid a hand on his arm. "Do your folks know how you feel?" Rick shrugged. "Well, maybe before you do anything else dangerous, you should try talking to them. If you don't, the anger will just get worse."

They were interrupted by the sound of a car door slamming. Charlie's parents, Rick's mother, and Joe came hurrying toward them.

"I called them before I came over," Alison said. "I was worried Rick might get hurt."

"I'm sure it would be his own fault if he were," Joe spat.

"Joe, please!" Rick's mother said, sounding weary.

"No, Mom, he's right." The two adults looked at Rick with surprise. "It was a dumb move to break into the skatepark. I guess I've been making a lot of dumb moves lately."

Joe opened his mouth to speak, but Rick cut him off.

"I know you think that extreme sports are dangerous and that I shouldn't be allowed to do them. But they're not dangerous, not as long as you obey some safety rules. If you would just give me half a chance, come see me ride sometime, you'd see that I know what I'm doing."

Charlie held his breath, waiting to see what Joe would say.

"Well, ahem," Joe finally said, clearing his throat. "I guess we can talk about it."

"In the meantime," Rick's mother said, "I'm afraid I will have to punish you for breaking into the skatepark. No Rocket Robert show for you tonight."

Rick didn't argue, but he shot Charlie a disappointed look.

Charlie threw an arm around his friend's shoulders – not an easy task, considering Rick was so

much taller. "I think I'll stay home, too. Alison, want two tickets to the show? Rick and I have a lot of catching up to do."

Rick stared at him, then broke into a big smile. "Yeah," he said. "I guess we do."

Charlie picked up his skateboard and started toward the park gate. "Um, Mom?" he said. "There's just one other thing I think you should know."

"Yes?" she said.

He held up a filthy stocking foot. "This pair of socks is shot."

They were all still laughing when they reached the gate.

"Hey, what's so funny?"

Outside the fence stood Jonas and X. Bizz, Savannah, and Mark were right behind them.

"So, what's the joke?" Jonas asked again.

"No joke," Charlie replied. "Guys, I'd like you to meet a friend of mine." He nudged Rick in the ribs. "We go way back. And you know what? I bet we're going to go way forward, too!"

A Short History of Skateboarding

Many people think skateboarding is a new sport, but it actually got its start nearly a century ago. In the early 1900s, children rode scooters made from an upright wooden crate with handles that was attached to a wooden plank on top of roller-skate wheels. Over the next few decades, changes were made to this crude design, the most important being improvements to the wheels. This change helped riders maneuver more easily. By the 1950s, the wooden crate and the handlebars had been abandoned and children simply rode on planks with wheels – the first true skateboards.

Skateboarding became very popular in the early 1960s. More than fifty million professionally made skateboards were sold from 1963 to 1965. Unfortunately, most of these skateboards featured cheap clay wheels that did not grip the pavement well. Riders often lost control of their boards, resulting in bad accidents. Reckless behavior also caused trouble. By late 1965, many cities had banned skateboarding, and the sport began to die out.

Then, in 1970, a surfer named Frank Nasworthy discovered that urethane wheels made for roller skates could also be used on skateboards. Urethane wheels worked much better than clay wheels, and when they replaced clay wheels in 1973, the sport of skateboarding took off once again.

Adventurous skateboarders took to riding in empty inground pools, leading to the birth of vert skating and the first skateparks. In 1978, when Alan Gelfand created the ollie – a simple move that popped the board into the air – streetstyle skating took on a whole new dimension. By the 1980s, both styles were hugely popular.

Skateboarding continues to grow and change.

Professional skateboarders like the amazing Tony Hawk are constantly working out new tricks, developing new-and-improved boards and equipment, and promoting skateboarding safety. Through their dedication, they launch themselves – and their sport – to ever greater heights.

THE eXTReme Team